Just Julia

A collection of short stories

by

Bernard Harvey

To Sheila with my dearest love Bernard x.

Published in 2015 by FeedARead.com publishing - Arts Council funded

Copyright © Bernard Harvey

First Edition

The author has asserted their moral right under the Copyright, Designs and Patents Act, 1988, to be identified as the author of this work.

All rights reserved. No part of this publication may be reproduced, copied, stored in a retrieval system, or transmitted, in any form or by any means, without the prior written consent of the copyright holder, nor be otherwise circulated in any form of binding or cover other than that in which it is published and without a similar condition being imposed on the subsequent purchaser.

The cover is taken from a painting by courtesy of www.claudmonetgallery.org

A CIP catalogue record for this title is available from the British Library.

Just Julia

Contents

Page	5	Foreword
Page	7	Julia and the lost spirit
Page	13	Julia and the brush strokes
Page	21	Julia and the hole in the ground
Page	27	Julia and the happy transvestite
Page	33	Julia and the montage
Page	39	Julia and the bequest
Page	49	Julia and the village fete
Page	55	Julia and the locked door mystery
Page	63	Julia and the rifleman
Page	71	Julia and the good deed
Page	79	Julia and the silence of Aphrodite

Just Julia

Foreword

This collection of short stories was brought about by writing *Julia and the silence of Aphrodite,* which won a prize in a competition run for Warminster Writers' Circle members.

The inspiration came from my neighbour, Pat, who runs a painting group and gave me the idea for stick painting, as well as other artistic ideas.

Writers' circles are a great way to inspire budding writers. Having been a member of Warminster Writers' Circle for about twenty years, I owe them a debt of gratitude for their encouragement; particularly David for reading the manuscript. The circle competitions are also a good way to try a genre that you would not normally attempt. Which is how *Just Julia* came about.

Julia is found in every village, town or city. She would never expect to become the source for a major novel; but would be the first to admit that most days in her life produce something of interest.

Bernard Harvey   March 2015

Julia and the lost spirit

Julia watched the removal van drive slowly away through the village of Upper Monksford, her new home. The lane was now empty except for an old man who was ambling slowly towards her. Curiosity kept her by the gate, for hers was the last cottage in the village and she wondered where he was heading.

'Afternoon missus.' His accent was West Country, possibly even Devonian.

Julia smiled. 'Hallo. It's very mild for October, isn't it?'

'Agh … 'tis November tomorrow.'

'So it is. I've just moved in.'

'Agh.'

' My name is Julia Philips. Do you live in the village?'

'Agh.'

'Can I help you? Er … I mean did you want to see me?'

'Ooh agh.'

'How can I help you?' By now Julia was beginning to think she was talking to herself.

'I used to do for Miss Tomkinson.'

'Miss … oh you mean the lady who lived here.'

'Agh. She died.'

'Yes, I know.' Julia added hastily. 'Just what did you do?'

'The garden, amongst other things.'

Julia nodded, not wanting to ask him to elaborate. 'I enjoy gardening,' she replied.

'Oh…'

'But I will need some help,' Julia added quickly. 'I'm sorry I don't know your name.'

'George.' He gazed up at the cottage. 'She's still here you know!'

'What! ... I mean who?'

'Miss Tomkinson.' George shook his head. 'They only found her body!'

Julia stared at the old man. 'Just what do you mean?'

'It's her spirit. It's still here.' He bent down and plucked a faded stalk of lavender. 'She loved her lavender bushes, that and her gin!' He turned to go. 'I'll be back tomorrow, after Halloween. She'll be quiet then!' With that he ambled back down the lane.

Still standing by the gate, Julia looked back at the cottage. It had been a good move. Since she had lost her husband in Afghanistan she was determined to rebuild her life. Her parents were happily retired on the South Coast and Robert's parents lived in Australia. The move to Upper Monksford seemed a bold move to the twenty-nine year old widow. But Julia Philips was built of stronger stuff.

By now it was half past four and as the clocks had gone back last weekend it was dusk. As she stared back at her new home she thought she saw something moving in one of the upstairs windows.

She shook her head. 'Don't be stupid, Julia. He's just a silly old man!' she muttered.

Back in the house Julia managed to light the wood burning stove and it was soon burning merrily. Settling down, she had just taken a sip of her tea and cut herself a slice of fruit cake when the jangle of the old fashioned front door bell startled her.

Crossing the hall she opened the front door 'Yes, can I heeeelp ...?' Julia's voice rose an octave and her hand flew to her mouth.

The four grotesque masks produced four little voices who replied in full pitch. 'Trick or treat!!'

'Oh ... oh you gave me such a start.' She paused. 'Of course it's Halloween. Now let me think. You see I only moved in today and I don't think I have anything handy ...'

The groan from the entourage was very audible. 'Trick ... trick ... trick ...trick,' they chanted.

'Wait!' commanded Julia and shut the door. It took her a few minutes, but she remembered the Mars bars she had bought for the workman and had forgotten! Relieved, she took them back to the front door. But when she opened it they had disappeared.

Suddenly Julia felt cold and with a shiver she shut the door and went back to the fire, but her tea too had gone cold. As she got up to get some more, the front door bell jangled again. With some irritation she grabbed the Mars bars and went back to the front door.

'I think that you might have waited ...' she stopped and regarded the familiar figure standing before her.

'Agh, thought you might like these.' George, resplendent in cords and a sweater, both of which had seen better days, held out a small bunch of dried lavender.

'Why thank you, George.' Surreptitiously Julia stuffed the Mars bars in her gilet and took the proffered offering.

'Just thought you needed some support. She be a bit bloody minded.'

'Really, who?'

'Miss Tomkinson! She takes a bit of getting used to. Just keep the gin locked up! So if it's alright I'll be here tomorrow?'

Julia recognised that this was one of the main reasons George had made a return. In good grace she replied, 'thank you, George. I look forward to seeing you then. And thank you for the lavender!'

George touched his cap and shuffled off towards the gate.

Julia went back into the house and put the dried lavender in a vase. She then rummaged in a box for a glass and, with a little more rummaging found a bottle of gin. It was a new bottle and she poured a liberal measure, added some tonic, before walking through to the kitchen to make a makeshift supper of scrambled eggs on toast. What with the long day, culminating with sitting in front of a warm fire, food and drink, Julia drifted slowly into dreamland.

Whether it was the television blaring out *Come Dancing*, or whether it was the bang on the ceiling, she wasn't sure. But whatever it was, she awoke with a start.

With some trepidation, Julia walked slowly up the stairs and hesitatingly opened the bedroom door. Slowly she slid her hand in to switch on the light. A sharp blast of cold air blew the door open. On the floor by a small table under the window was a broken gin bottle. As Julia watched, a glass spun from the table and crashed to the floor beside the bottle.

Julia gave out a small squeak, then shook her head. 'Don't be stupid, Julia,' she muttered as she walked firmly across to the window, which was wide open. With her heart pounding, she pulled the window shut and left the room slamming the door behind her.

Surprisingly, Julia slept well. For the first of November the day dawned bright and sunlight lit the garden, which was looking rather bedraggled. The trees were like bare fingers reaching to the sky, their cast off clothing strewn in brown patches across the lawn. Carrying a mug of coffee, Julia walked out and regarded the overgrown borders. As she turned back towards the back door, George shambled around the corner of the house.

'Mornin' missus. Where would you like me to start?'

'Good morning, George. You're bright and early.'

'Agh well, Miss T was a right stickler for time keeping. Unless she'd been on the gin!'

'Fine, well if you could start with all the leaves on the lawn.' Leaving George to it, Julia went back in the house and decided to unpack some of the boxes in the living room. She started on the glasses and put them in the corner cupboard, together with the bottles. It was as she placed the latter away she suddenly noticed that the gin bottle was nearly empty.

Puzzled, Julia held the bottle up to the light. 'Extraordinary, I opened a new bottle last night and only had a large one. But not that large!' she muttered. A tap on the window made her jump. Julia went over and opened it.

'Yes, what is it, George?' she called.

'I warned you. She does like her gin!' George nodding towards the bottle Julia held in her hand.

'Don't talk rubbish!'

'Talking of which missus, do you want me to burn the leaves?'

'Yes, thank you, George.' Julia put the gin in the cupboard and looked round to see if there were any tonics, before remembering that she had left a half empty bottle on the small table behind the lavender George had brought her. It was there with a nearly full bottle of gin, bathed in an aroma of lavender - she smiled - 'Ah the lost spirit!'

Julia and the brush strokes

Julia stood in front of her class of adult students and took a deep breath. 'Good evening everyone. My name is Julia Philips I am your new art teacher, following the sad death of Mr. Thomas. For the time being, I suggest that you carry on with your own projects. However, I have found that it helps before we all start painting, just to reflect on one aspect of our work. Tonight I want to talk about *brush strokes*.'

St. Mary's bells rang out to call the good people of Upper Monksford to morning service. It was a cold late February morning, but the sun was up and with a promise of a warmer day to come. Julia Philips abandoned her catalogues and notes to get ready and join the local congregation. Not that she was a regular church goer, but meeting the Vicar whilst out for a walk yesterday had tweaked her conscience.

It had been nearly a year since the death of her husband, Robert, and she had recently moved into Manor Cottage. But now she decided she needed a studio and so her kitchen table was littered with ideas for a studio cum summerhouse in the garden.

'Good morning, Julia. It's nice to see you.' Archie Thursfield, Vicar of St Mary's, held out his hand to Julia.

'Thank you, Vicar.'

'No. Thank you for coming and please, no-one calls me vicar, except the postman. Archie is my name.' He smiled.

'Archie is a bonus to the community.' The speaker was a well dressed lady in her mid fifties, who was following Julia out of the church.

'Ah, good morning, Lady Berwick.' Archie turned and introduced her to Julia. 'Lady Florence is our good Samaritan, who turns her hand to everything. Particularly allowing us to use the Manor gardens for our village fete. Now if you will excuse me I must have a word with old Mr. Walker.'

As Julia turned to walk down the church path, Lady Florence Berwick touched her arm.

'It was very rude of me, but I should have welcomed you to the village. Especially as you now have Manor Cottage.'

Julia smiled. 'Thank you. I'm afraid I haven't had time to get out and explore very much.' She regarded the lady who strolled beside her. A lady in her mid fifties she thought, her dark hair beginning to show a little grey and with an attractive face.

'You must come to tea, how about next Thursday at four?'

It sounded more like a summons than an invitation, but Julia could never be called faint hearted and she nodded.

'Good. Well this is where I go the other way. I'm glad we met!' With a wave, Lady Berwick turned and carried on walking through the village.

The Manor was set well back from the road, but it had a delightful drive bordered by mostly lawn, covered with masses of snowdrops. A track went round to the side of the manor house where, later, Julia discovered a large orchard which backed on to her garden.

Lady Berwick answered the door herself and ushered Julia through to the drawing room where a fire burned in the large hearth. 'This is my favourite room in the winter, probably because it is the warmest room in the house,' she explained.

'What a delightful outlook, it must be lovely in the summer. Especially with the French doors opening out on to such a great vista.'

Lady Berwick smiled. 'You are quite right. This is where I do all my correspondence and I am an avid reader.' She waved a hand at the ample bookshelves. 'Now, tea! In the afternoon I always have a mixture of Lady Grey and common or garden breakfast tea, I hope you approve. Come and sit by the fire.' The tea things were already laid out. She accepted her tea and a shortbread biscuit as her hostess announced that they had something in common.

'How interesting,' Julia replied, her curiosity aroused.

'Sadly it is. You see I lost my brother, also killed in action.' She sat down opposite Julia and folded her hands in her lap. 'John was killed in the Falklands war. He was just twenty-seven, a newly gazetted captain. I was just nineteen, he was my hero.'

Julia stared for a few seconds and then remembered where she was. 'I'm so sorry.' she stammered. 'But how did you know I had lost my husband?'

'They were in the same regiment. An old friend who is now the Adjutant, saw your change of address and put two and two together.' She smiled. 'You know what the army is like!'

Julia relaxed and smiled back. 'Well I didn't really get a chance to find out, as I was teaching when

Robert was killed in Afghanistan. His parents lived in Australia and I decided to start anew.'

Lady Berwick sipped her tea and poised for a second, holding the cup in front of her, whilst regarding her guest. 'What did you teach?'

' I taught art at a girl's school.'

'I apologise if I have got it wrong, but I was also informed that you have had a painting hung in the Tate Gallery.'

Julia blushed. 'That was two years ago. I entered a competition for fun and won. One of the conditions was, that the winner would be submitted to the Royal Acadamy Open Exhibition for acceptance. And it was!'

'Will you continue to paint?'

Julia laughed. 'I hope to. I had planned to have a studio in my garden. That is until I saw the costs. Maybe I shall have to go back to teaching.'

The following week, Julia was sitting in her kitchen and staring out into her garden. It wasn't as though she was financially stretched, but she knew that in a year or two her budget would have to be cut, unless she had an earned income. She had her widow's pension from the army but inwardly she knew that if she painted full time, it still wouldn't be enough.

At that moment George appeared at the kitchen door. George was her gardener and odd job man. At 81, George didn't move too quickly, but he couldn't start the day without a cup of coffee and a chocolate digestive biscuit.

'Good morning, George. How are you today?' Julia realised that from the first morning he appeared, it was a mistake to ask him that question; but it had become a habit and in a perverse sort of way she waited for his daily health report.

'It's in my thumbs, Missus,' he replied. 'Agh ... both of them.'

'Sorry to hear that, George. Coffee?'

'Ooh agh.'

'Biscuit?'

'Ooh agh.'

'By the way, what IS in your thumbs, George?' Julia carried on getting his refreshments and then carried them across to the stable door, where he was standing.

'Tis arferitus,' he announced firmly. 'I inherited it from my granddad, he caught it in the war.'

Julia fell for it again. 'Which war, George?'

'Agh well ...'. At that moment the phone rang.

'Hello Julia, this is Florence Berwick.'

'Lady Berwick, how can I help you?'

'Please call me Florence. After all we are neighbours and I do hope we shall be good friends.'

'That is very kind of you, but I am still not sure why you called me?'

'Well it is a bit of a coincidence, but I was at a luncheon yesterday evening and I met the Principal of the College in Pencastle, Stephen Fenwick. He was bemoaning the cuts in their budget, but his biggest worry at the moment is the sad accident to his Head of the Art department. So I took the liberty of giving him your name as a possible replacement. I hope you don't mind?'

'My name! I have only taught at a girl's school, never as a college lecturer!'

'Well, to be honest, it is a college of Further

Education and the principle classes are for adult vocation, although I do understand they run Foundation courses.' Lady Berwick paused for a second. 'I thought the adult courses would be right up your street, especially as it should give you time to paint.'

Two weeks later Julia decided to visit Lady Berwick, with a small gift as a thank you. She walked up the drive to the front of the manor house, where she stopped at the front door and pulled on the bell. Somewhere in the house she heard it jangle above the continuous cry of the rooks which swirled overhead.

The house was quiet and Julia waited patiently for several minutes. She was just about to walk away when the door was opened by an elderly man. He stood for a second regarding his visitor and then barked 'Yes?'

Julia looked startled. 'I'm sorry, I wondered if I could speak to Lady Berwick?'

'What?'

'Um ... I asked if I could see ...' Julia replied hesitatingly.

'Yes .. yes I heard what you said. I'm not deaf you know! My wife thinks I am, but I can hear perfectly well.'

Julia realised that this must be Sir Harry Berwick. 'My name is Julia Philips.'

'Philip? Damned strange name for a girl. Well you had better come in.' He tottered the way to the drawing room.

Opening the door, he announced Julia as if she was going ten rounds with Frank Bruno.

'Julia! How nice of you to call. Now you will

stay and have some coffee. Julia nodded.

'Come and sit by the fire.' Then raising her voice she said 'Harry, will you ask Dorry to make some coffee?

Muttering her husband closed the door behind him.

Julia sat herself down opposite Lady Berwick and they made small talk until the door opened and a plump jolly looking woman appeared carrying a tray of coffee things, which she set down on a small table by her mistress.

'How are you getting on with your classes?' Florence asked as she passed Julia a cup of coffee.

'Very well, I think. At least they seemed happy with me. It is quite easy really as I let them carry on with their current project. But I did give them some food for thought.'

'How interesting! What does that entail?'

'Well it is simple really. I just offer a tip on one aspect of their work before each class. Although this time it was more like half a dozen tips rolled into one; just to follow the rules of *brush strokes*. Such as - use a variety of strokes - don't be stingy with the paint - mix the paint on your palette, not on the canvas - and so on.' Julia paused, half embarrassed.

'Please carry on, I'm intrigued,' Florence said.

'Well, *brush strokes* are the same as handwriting. In fact they can usually identify the artist. They can now do a computerised analysis of an individual's *brush strokes*. For example an expert can take a piece of art and comparing them with known and named works they can identify the artist.'

It was probably three months later when Julia

was watching The Antiques Road Show and to her surprise there was her neighbour, Lady Florence Berwick.

She was holding a small oil painting, which she passed over to the expert. He turned it over and over, examining it this way and that. Then with a little smug smile of satisfaction, he excitedly announced that indeed it could be quite valuable. But as usual it would have to be put through various tests. He looked up at Lady Florence. 'What on earth gave you an idea that it could be the work of an old master? This could have been missed by many a well known expert,' he enquired.

Lady Florence smiled. 'Simply a very good friend said I should check the *brush strokes*!'

Julia and the hole in the ground

It didn't bode well for a peaceful weekend when, on the Saturday morning, Julia looked out of her bedroom window and found the lower part of her beloved garden totally flooded.

Water flowed across the lawn through the rose garden, down through the shrubbery and was building a small lake under the oak trees. Julia grabbed the phone and dialled a local number.

'George, thank God you're in!' Julia paused and took a deep breath. 'It's Julia. Julia Philips at Manor Cottage.'

'Ahhhh.'

'George are you there?'

'Ahhhh!'

'I'm in desperate need of your help.'

'Oh?'

'There's water pouring through my garden from the lane.'

'Oh!'

'Can you come and have a look?'

'Bit difficult, like!'

'Why? George I am desperate.'

'Well you may not like it. Cos I'm in the bath with my ferrets.'

Julia shrieked. 'George ... I don't want to know what you do in the bath, but I need help now!'

'Ah, well I don't want them to catch cold like. They'm very funny things ferrets. But I'll be along shortly. Mind you, young Blondie looks a treat, I've high hopes for the Agriculture Show next week. She's a right beauty, bit of a killer though…'

Julia put down the phone without waiting to hear about Blondie's attributes. A mug of coffee later she heard her side gate click and George appeared. If there was anyone in the village who had more knowledge of the local water supply, then Julia had yet to meet them. They made their way across the lawn to where the water was flowing through the hedge from the bridle way.

'Ahhhh.' The font of all knowledge stood and scratched his head and then his bottom.

Julia raised her eyes to the sky and tried hard not to watch.

'Tis the junction, gorn again!'

'What junction?' Julia stared at the water flowing freely from what appeared to be a large hole in the ground. 'What do you mean, gone again?'

'Well it happened a while back. 1978, I think!' George scratched down the front of his trousers and then chuckled as he hauled out a small blonde ferret.

'Oh my God.' Julia blanched and put her hand over her mouth.

'This is Blondie… a beauty isn't she? You'm nice and dry and warm down there. Mind you, it does tickle the old man a bit!'

'George!'

'Sorry missus.' He stuffed the ferret into his jacket pocket. 'Right I'll ring Fred and ask him to turn the water off, he should have milked by now. I'll be back with some tools.' He ambled off down the bridle way.

Julia sighed and after another glance at the steady flow of water wandered back into the house. After all there was nothing she could do so she might as well get some breakfast.

It was a good two hours later, after the water had stopped flowing, when Julia heard a knock at the back door. Opening it she was confronted by an ashen faced George.
'Why whatever is the matter, George?'
Standing wringing his hands in front him George shuffled his feet. 'You'm better come and have a look, missus.' Without waiting for a reply he turned and walked back to the lane.
Puzzled, she followed him and when they got to his excavations, George silently pointed down into the trench. Julia peered over into the muddy hole which was partly filled with water. There neatly turned over on a spit of soil was a complete human scull. The water had washed it clean and the dark eye sockets stared broodingly up at her.

By lunchtime the police and their forensic team had blocked off the lane and set up a large tent over George's hole.
By teatime all the village were agog and Julia was quite surprised by the number of offers she got when they heard about her lack of water supply. She politely turned down George's offer of the use of his bath, although he did assure her the ferrets wouldn't be in sight. Julia wasn't so sure about George though!
By evening The Stags Head was packed, especially when rumours started to fly; the local press had arrived and *All Points West* did a brief interview with George in the pub car park.
By next morning George had a hangover.

It took nearly a week for the police to complete their investigation and the village was awash with rumours, whilst Julia was unable to wash at all; so in desperate need of a more civilised living she went to stay with her cousin, Jean, in Bristol.

On the Thursday she received a call on her mobile, it was the local inspector. She could return to her cottage as the water supply had been reconnected, but more to the point, forensic discovered enough clues not only to determine the age and sex of the body, but from his dog tag he was identified as a soldier who had disappeared in 1942. Apparently there had been a fight at The Stags Head, when the soldier had been accused of assaulting a local lad's girl friend. They had gone outside to settle the matter when they were caught up in a heavy air raid. The local lad was found dead, the next morning. Killed it was assumed by a piece of shrapnel in his head; but of the soldier there was no sign and the whole affair remained a mystery. That is until he turned up in the hole in the lane opposite Julia's cottage, some fifty odd years later.

It was several months when the dust had settled, so to speak, and the coroner had given an open verdict on the body as - *death by a hand unknown* - Julia was relaxing in her Summer House enjoying the Sunday papers, when she heard her front gate click. Cursing gently, she called out to her visitor. To her surprise, George Ploughman made his way down the garden path towards the Summer House.

'Why hello, George, what brings you round on a Sunday?'

'Er, can you spare few minutes, Miss Philips?'
'Of course, would you like some tea, George?'
'No thank you, Missus.'

'Have a seat.'

'No thank you, Missus.'

'Well?' Julia folded up her newspaper and looked up at George expectantly.

'It's about that body.'

Julia took a deep breath. 'Yes?'

'T'wernt an accident!'

'What do you mean?'

'Young Fred. That soldier knocked him down and he hit his head on the step, just before the bombs fell and a then a large piece of shrapnel hit Fred within seconds. He could have been dead before the shrapnel hit him.'

'You don't know that, George.' Julia added quietly.

'Oh we did, there was a witness.'

'Who?'

'Fred's girl, Lucy. She had gone to The Stags Head that night to meet Fred. Being only fifteen, she couldn't go in. To her horror she saw the fight.'

'What happened?'

'Several local lads confronted the soldier later that night near the farm where he was billeted.'

'And you, George. You were one of the local lads?'

George stared at the ground for some seconds, before nodding. 'Lucy was my younger sister, I would do anything for her.'

Julia covered her mouth briefly with her hand. After a second or two she whispered. 'What did you do?'

'Nothing.'

'Nothing?'

'We didn't have to.' George paused 'Lucy

arrived and pulled out a .410 shotgun from under a coat she was carrying, aiming it at the man's chest she pulled the trigger.'

'Oh my God.' Julia once again covered her mouth.

'Some of the lads got rid of the body as I took Lucy home.'

'And Lucy?'

'She married an American serviceman three years later and now lives happily in Texas with her five children and eleven grandchildren and seven great grandchildren at the last count.'

Julia shook her head 'Why have you told me this, George?'

'I'm eighty-one this year and the doc says I haven't got long, maybe a couple of years. An' before I go I want to make sure someone knows the truth. T'weren't Lucy's fault, I blame the war, it changes people. Some never recover, but some like Lucy are forgiven and find true happiness.'

Julia and the happy transvestite

Sean O'Connor had a wicked sense of humour, which came to the fore especially when he was confronted by an immovable object. In this case the immovable object was Mrs Pamela Speak-Patterson.

It was on a Wednesday evening, when he attended Julia Philips' art class, which as usual was held at the college of Further Education in Pencastle. As they had their break for coffee, Julia read out some notices she thought might be of interest to her students. One of which concerned an art competition for amateur artists, which was being held in the neighbouring town of Ketton.
'I think that this may be a great opportunity for several of you to submit your work. It must not of course have won any prizes in any competitions before and ....' At this point Julia was interrupted by one of her class.
'You may have forgotten that it is for ladies only,' boomed Mrs Pamela Speak-Patterson.
'Ah.' Julia glanced at the leaflet she was holding. 'Yes... yes I'm afraid it does preclude you chaps.' She smiled at the few men who were members of her class.
'Sheer sexism!' announced Sean.
'I don't think that it is meant in any way,' placated Julia.
'Not what you would say if it was for men only,' he retaliated.

'As a member of Ketton Ladies Art Society, I can honestly say that we can quite well do without some of the chauvinistic painters we find littering the countryside,' came the stentorian voice of Mrs PSP. 'They drink too much and as for their morals.'

'I hope that you're not referring to me.'

'If the cap fits..'

Julia moved the subject quickly on, reading out an offer for art materials she had received in the post; but at the same time keeping an eye on Sean, who was glowering at Mrs PSP, who in turn looked as smug as an over blown peony.

After the class and as they were clearing up Julia was surprised when Sean asked to see the leaflet from Ketton Ladies Art Society.

'It's no good, Sean,' she said as she passed across the leaflet, 'they present the prizes in person.'

'Mm.. pity though, the one on wildlife would be right up my street!'

Julia had to agree. Some of his paintings of badgers had been quite stunning.

'Maybe, I'll try a nom de plume,'

She shook her head 'No, Sean. I don't think it would work.'

The seed of devilment that had been planted in Sean's mind that evening now began to germinate and by the time he had drunk a couple of pints of Kestrel Real Ale down at the Dirty Duck he knew what he was going to do.

The Ketton Ladies Art Society held its meetings in Ketton Town Hall. It was a very formal and grand affair, with Lady C as president and the Honourable Mrs Uppingham acting as chair. Surrounded by her committee, which of course included Mrs Pamela Speak-Patterson,the chairlady, she rose to introduce their guest.

'Ladies, we are so lucky this year, to have as our guest speaker and competition judge, the most distinguished and universally known member of the Royal Academy....' she paused for effect. 'Sir Aubrey Fotheringay'

Her introduction was greeted by an enthusiastic audience of some fifty woman who had crammed into what was the Town Council Chamber.

If Sir Aubrey seemed intimidated by such a large assembly of the opposite sex, it didn't seem to bother him. In a quiet, slightly effeminate voice, he thanked the chair and briefly touched on the work by the Royal Academy with particular reference to its support for the amateur. He then explained the division of the various classes in the competition and praised the Society on its depth of talent. He went on to present the prizes. When he got to the best wildlife picture in any medium, he paused. It was, he explained, only once or twice in his lifetime that he had come across a new artist's work that excited him as much as the winner of this class had done.

'It is with the greatest of pleasure that I award the first prize and Ketton Ladies Art Society Cup for a most outstanding piece of work to...' he glanced at his notes, 'Miss Mollie Malone.'

For a several seconds there was a look of puzzlement on the faces of the Hon. Mrs Uppingham and her Committee, which only changed to blank looks as a tall angular lady wearing a colourful kaftan and a matching headscarf tied around her head, rose to her feet and made her way up to receive her award.

Sir Aubrey passed over the envelope containing a cheque and her certificate. Shaking her hand he congratulated her and still holding her hand he lifted the cup which was immediately photographed by a member of the local press.

The Hon. Mrs Uppingham hurriedly conferred with her committee. It appeared that Miss Malone was a fully paid up member of their Society.

As the meeting started to break up, The Hon. Mrs Uppingham cornered the new member who was clutching a glass of wine.

'We haven't met before. I'm Marjorie Uppingham.'

The new member shyly smiled and replied in a slightly squeaky voice. 'Hello.'

'Sir Aubrey was most impressed with your work. I'm just surprised I haven't seen you at any meetings.'

'Just moved here,' squeaked Miss Malone, nodding her head, leaving the Hon. Mrs Uppingham lost for words.

'Strange woman,' boomed a voice in her ear. She turned to find Mrs PSP staring at Miss Malone's retreating figure.

'Mmm… Find out what you can, Pamela, old girl.'

Her cohort nodded and weaved with some difficulty after the elusive Miss Malone.

Sean O'Connor was finding this charade more difficult than he thought. More to the point he was sure that Mrs PSP was suspicious that Miss Malone was not all she may appear to be under the surface. Several of the ladies had spilled out of the claustrophobic atmosphere of the Chamber and were standing chatting in the corridor. Finishing his wine Sean O'Connor, aka Miss Malone, felt in urgent need of finding a toilet and it was with some relief that he saw the sign and hurried through the door.

It is said that Confucious wrote *'rape is impossible - as woman with skirt up can run faster than man with trousers down.'* The saying came to mind as confronted with a urinal. Sean smiled and lifted his skirt.

Breathing a sigh of relief, Sean literally adjusted his dress and opened the men's toilet door. He was confronted by a horrified crowd of ladies who lined the corridor making way for a thunderous looking chairlady and a smug looking Mrs Pamela Speak-Patterson.

'What,' glared the Hon Mrs Uppingham, 'do you think you are doing in there?'

'It's him,' trumped her cohort. 'It's him!'

'What do you mean, him?' she replied.

'That's Sean what's his name, ' announced Mrs PSP

'You mean HE's a woman?' The Hon. Mrs Uppingham was finding this all to much.

'No a man!' She hissed, 'he's one of those, a trans... trans-sexuals!'

There was an audible sigh in the corridor and The Honourable Lady clutched her bosom as if she was protecting it from something nasty.

'Transvestite, Madam, Transvestite!'

The corridor swung their heads like Wimbledon as Sir Aubrey made his way towards them. 'He just likes dressing up - don't we all, ladies?'

'I can explain... ' Sean's explanation was cut

short as an outraged Honourable Mrs Uppingham snatched the cup from under his arm and stormed back to the chamber, followed by her entourage.

Sir Aubrey draped an arm a little too affectionately around Sean's shoulder 'Young man, I meant what I said - you have great talent, including your choice in clothes!' He fished in his pocket and took out a business card. 'Now call me next week and we will have a nice little lunch together whilst we discuss your future.' Patting Sean's cheek he walked off down the now empty corridor towards the exit.

Sean stared after him and thrust his hands into the pockets of the dress. Feeling the envelope Sir Aubrey had presented him just a few minutes ago, he pulled it out and opened it, gazing at the cheque for £100. Sean smiled happily and kissed the cheque, but silently he wondered if Julia Philips would agree.

Julia and the Montage

Julia sat bathed in candlelight, reflected by the polished Victorian mahogany table and observed her five friends with the kind of satisfied pleasure one derives from hosting an excellent dinner party.

She had to admit the choice of friends was a good mix. Two friends who were members of her adult art class, together with their husbands, whilst the fifth guest was Tom Ryder an occasional student at her classes and who was a neighbour.

The coffee had been served and their conversation had ranged from the play *Vincent in Brixton* to the fire that virtually destroyed the Cutty Sark, when Tom brought up the subject of her latest class exercise - a montage of past memories.

The result had been a huge cross section of nostalgia, world and local events, love won and love lost; these were presented in a variety of ways and although artistically not outstanding, it had proved a good workshop.

'I must say I thought that Rula's entry was a bit startling,' commented Tom.

Sheila put down her coffee cup. 'Using the mythological story of Minos and the white bull? I think she was trying tell us something!'

'What on earth do you mean?' Richard, her husband stared across at her over the table. 'If I remember rightly Minos's wife fell in love with a white bull and managed to get pregnant; although God knows how. I do remember at school we debated all sorts of bestial ways.'

Sheila raised her eyes to the ceiling. 'I think what she was doing was trying to lay ghosts to rest.'

'That's a bit far fetched,' commented Diana doubtingly.

'Why? Julia asked us to be completely free with our interpretations,' she replied looking at Julia for corroboration.

Julia nodded. To tell the truth she hadn't got round to look at Rula's work at the end of the last session.

Tom stepped in to cover her embarrassment and asked if he could have some more coffee. The subject was passed over and Julia might have forgotten it if it hadn't been for the news that broke that weekend. Rula Clowski had been found dead in the London flat of a wealthy Russian businessman.

On Wednesday, as usual the class slowly filled up and between setting up the easels and starting work, the subject of Rula was debated with a sordid interest. Especially as one student had seen a report of the death in one of the more lurid Sunday papers.

Julia suddenly remembered the story related by Sheila. Going into the small side room where they stored their work she searched until she found Rula's montage and carried it out into the better light.

It was divided into five individual pictures each set in a cloud like background connected by wisps of blue sky. As Julia stared at the picture a voice at her shoulder made her jump. 'I did say startling!' She turned to find Tom staring at the picture.

'Mm... what do you think it means?'

'Well it looks like a story, you said memories,

but this could be a nightmare. It starts in the top left hand corner and the rosebud on a pillow with a teddy bear could represent a child or a young girl...' Tom paused and Julia interrupted him. 'Look, I need to get the class under way, why don't we go for a drink later and discuss it then?'

As it happened they ended up in Tom's cottage, which was within walking distance of Julia's house. It was still just light as he led the way through to his conservatory. 'What would you like to drink?'
'Red wine would be lovely.'
'OK. Have a seat and I'll be with you in a minute.'
A few minutes later seated with a glass of wine Julia held a book that she had picked up from the table beside her chair. 'I didn't know you were in the police force. What's this book, *A Last Case* by Inspector Tom Ryder?'
Looking a bit sheepish Tom took a sip of wine. 'I decided to put into print my last case which was nearly the last of me! I cornered this villain we had been watching for months and he pulled out a gun and fired. I was lucky, off for six months, but when I went back I spent some time working on our crime databases before realising that I had no heart in it and took early retirement.'
'Well Inspector, what do you think of this?' Julia smiled as she pulled Rula's picture out of a plastic portmanteau. They both pored over the painting until Tom leaned back and picked up his wine glass.
'Tell me what you see picture by picture, follow the ribbon of blue, starting in the top left hand quarter.'
Julia took a deep breath. 'Well... the first

picture of the rosebud on a pillow is representing not a girl but I believe it to be of a young woman, probably single and could be a teenager. The second is a still life showing the top of an antique desk which has what appears to be a legal document torn in half, a half smoked cigar viciously stubbed out in an ashtray and a whisky glass on its side with a spilt pool of liquid. The third is the central picture with a white bull emerging from the sea. The fourth picture is again a still life showing what looks like a negligee draped over the end of a bed with rose petals strewn around. Whilst the last picture is bizarre..' Julia paused and then continued, 'a road across a meadow of flowers, going up to a dark wood, where it abruptly stops.'

Tom nodded and got up to turn on some side lights which accentuated the end of the summer's day. Julia shuddered as she glanced at the darkened windows.

'Five pictures that tell a story and lead to the death of a woman.'

'That sounds a bit melodramatic,' replied Julia.

'She may not have known it would do so, but I think she had an inkling of what was to come.' Tom picked up the bottle of wine and topped up their glasses. He continued. ' Now let me sum up for each of the pictures and you tell me if you think I'm wrong. It starts with a young woman, secondly we have a torn or broken contract causing anger and followed by the appearance of a white bull which makes me think of Minos in Greek Mythology. Let's just suppose that Rula married and her husband double crossed someone else and, as in the mythological story, sent in a bull or third party. He was handsome and either Rula fell in love or was seduced or even raped - look at the negligee, how its torn. This lead Rula to believe that there was no future - her road lead to a dead end - a dark wood and possibly even death.'

Julia regarded Tom with amazement. 'Extraordinary, how do you do it!'

'Do what?'

'Have such an imagination!'

Tom grinned. 'Probably fuelled by my art teacher!'

It was next Saturday morning and Julia was busy in her garden when she heard the garden gate latch. 'Oh good morning Tom, good timing, I was just about to stop for coffee.'

When they had settled themselves on a garden bench with mugs of coffee and chocolate digestives, Tom could contain himself no longer. 'You will be pleased to hear that we are expecting an arrest any moment!'

'I thought you had retired!'

'Well I had, but I still have many contacts in the Met and my or rather our theories on Rula and the motive for her death appears to have been taken seriously.'

'Really? How exciting, do tell.'

'We were right up to a point - apparently Rula was a beauty and married quite young to a Russian business man. It turns out the man was a bit of a rogue and conned his partner into buying forward on the market in other words trading in bulls. But the stock turned out to be worthless so when he had to settle up, he lost all his money. The partner was incensed as you can imagine, so he decided to get his own back. The rumour is, he used the date-rape drug, and poor Rula fell victim to some young Lothario. From then on she was blackmailed into working for the man, until in desperation she left her husband and found some solace down in this part of the world.'

'Then why go back?'

'For some odd reason, she fell in love with her seducer, but it all came to light as the flat she died in belonged to the partner who decided that she had renegaded on their deal. A messy business.'

Julia gazed at her roses 'Indeed. Not what I had in mind when I set the exercise!'

Julia and the bequest

Uncle Henry had been one of the old school. Sadly, Julia sat silently as with a bewildering collection of other family and friends they listened to the local rector extol the virtues of Henry Eisenhower Montgomery Wilberforce, late of that parish.

It appears that when he had been in residence, he had been a generous friend to his local church, chairman and benefactor of the local cricket club, vice-president of the local history society and president of the local arts society. In fact the list seemed endless and Julia's sadness wavered as she realised that she had never realised how embroiled in local life her uncle had become.

Life had dealt him a poor hand when his wife had been taken prematurely in their married life, and childless he had thrown himself into village life. That is, when he wasn't travelling abroad, which was quite often as he had a villa in the South of France.

When in residence in his house in the village of Nether Watchet, he would invite his niece to stay. On Saturdays it would be a trip to Bath, lunch at the Francis Hotel, shopping and then back to the Francis for tea before adjourning around the corner to the Theatre Royal.

The service, which had moved outside to the churchyard for the burial, came to a close. Julia, having thanked the Rector for his kind words, walked across the village street to the Swan Hotel where her parents and other relatives had arranged some refreshments. As she stood talking to a lady who turned out to be the clerk to the parish council she was aware of her mother joining her.

'Julia, dear.' Her mother smiled at the clerk to the council and excusing herself guided her daughter away by her elbow.

'Mother! Whatever is the matter, that was extremely rude to that poor lady.'

'I'm sorry dear but I must speak to you before your father puts in his tuppence worth.'

Julia sighed, she loved her parents dearly, but they did have opposing views on things which sometimes, no matter how trivial, caused mayhem in the family.

'The point is,' hissed her mother, 'I don't think you should accept. Don't listen to your father, you know how he can be so obstinate in these matters. I remember when he tried to insist on you following in his footsteps, I mean one solicitor in the family is bad enough.'

'Fine, mother,' Julia smiled, 'of course, whatever you say, but I think it may be easier if I knew what on earth you are talking about.'

'Your Uncle Henry, ' Julia's mother hissed.

'Mother. 'Julia's patience was beginning to wear a little thin.

Her mother took Julia's arm and turning her to face across the room nodded at a youngish woman talking to the Rector. 'Her!' she hissed.

Julia regarded the elegant woman who with beautiful milk chocolate features was smiling at a young girl aged about twelve who stood quietly between herself and the Rector. Her view was interrupted as her father hove into view accompanied by another man whom Julia recognised as one of her father's partners in Wilberforce & Portly Solicitors.

'Ah Julia, we would like a quiet word.'

Quite used to father's quiet words Julia kissed him on the cheek and whispered in his ear 'Not now father. Come round for supper on Friday.' Without waiting for a reply she kissed her mother and left the reception.

Driving back to her own home, Julia reflected on her Uncle and how much she would miss him. His treats had been more common in her late teens and early twenties, but as she grew older and when she married, his contacts became rarer and yet always generous on her birthday and at Christmas when she would receive a delightful note apologising for his absence but enclosing a substantial cheque. Since her husband died, Uncle Henry had invited her to stay with him in France, but sadly she had never been in a position when she seemed able to accept.

Friday evening came and Julia tactfully allowed an extra hour before supper for whatever it was her father wished to talk about. As it happens, the weather was still warm and they spent the time admiring the garden until Julia's curiosity got the better of her.

'Now come on Dad, spit it out. You been hedging ever since you got here!'

'Julia, have you got some more ice?' Her mother looked flustered.

'Why yes ...'

'No you stay and talk to your father. I'll find it!'

Julia raised an eyebrow and sat down on her favourite garden seat opposite Aphrodite. 'Well?' she asked.

Mr Wilberforce stood clutching his whisky and took a deep breath. 'My brother Henry was a very generous man.' He paused and took a large swig of his drink. 'However in latter years he was prone to making some, shall we say, unorthodox gestures.'

'What sort of gestures?'

'Like, well... Oh damn it, Julia ... your Uncle was proposing to get married.'

Julia giggled 'Dad, what is unorthodox about that? He was probably lonely and wanted some company.'

'Yes, well she happened to be a thirty three years old model and he was sixty seven! She was young enough to be his daughter!'

'So?'

John Wilberforce glanced at his daughter then finished his drink before answering, 'She's the Ethiopian woman at the funeral with the young girl.'

'Is she his child?'

'What? Her father snapped 'I don't bloody know.'

For the second time in succession Julia raised her eyebrows - it was truly rare for her father to lose his cool.

He continued. 'We don't know. But he must have thought so, because he has left a large bequest in trust for them both.'

Julia nodded. 'Well as far as I can see, Uncle Henry has no other children and maybe she gave him a lot of pleasure.' She blushed. 'Having a daughter, I mean.'

John Wilberforce apparently failed to take in the *double entendre* and carried on. ' The trust has three trustees, my colleague Robert Farmer, a French solicitor and the other… is you!'

'Me!' Julia stood up. 'Why me?'

'Well it's not as easy as that.' Henry added a proviso, 'we understand that he requested that you were to manage the trust.'

Julia sat down again. She was speechless.

Her father, forever the family solicitor, never the affectionate relaxed father, coughed diplomatically. 'Julia, there's more!'

'More!' Julia exploded. 'What was Uncle Henry thinking of?'

'Well he also asked me to give you this letter.'

Julia took the envelope her father handed to her and opening it she took out the single sheet of notepaper, it was addressed from his villa in Antibes.

My dear Julia,
By the time you read this I will be away with the fairies, not a time to be sad, I have enjoyed every moment.
What I do now, I do knowing that you of all of my family will understand my actions.
I met Mahilia when she was twenty-two. She was alone in   Paris and we became close friends. Over the years I have   enjoyed a   friendship which has been blessed with a beautiful daughter, Lucille.
I have sufficient funds for her schooling and living expenses which are paid into her mothers account every month. If anything should happen to her mother, I would ask that you apply to become her guardian. In return I hope that you will accept my gift. Details of which you will find from my Paris solicitors at the address enclosed.

43

My very grateful thanks.
Always your loving uncle
Henry

Julia dipped into the envelope and pulled out a business card of the solicitors in Paris. She gazed at it blindly before returning it to the envelope along with the letter. 'Did you know what the contents contained?' she asked her father.

He shook his head.

'This is unreal.' She gave a brief outline and continued. 'What do I do?'

Her father shook his head. 'Julia, I am at a loss to answer.'

Julia took a large swig from a glass of wine she had set down on the garden table earlier. 'Well, it will have to wait. I suppose a trip to Paris is the next step.'

At nearly thirty years of age Julia considered herself still a young woman. So when she booked herself a ticket on the Eurostar to Paris it was with a tinge of sadness. The last time she visited the city of romance she had been twenty three and on her honeymoon.

However, by the time she reached Euston station she had felt that little buzz every traveller has when they are about to leave their day to day life behind. In fact she tried to remember when it was she had last travelled abroad. Was it really three years ago? She and her best friend, Celia, had spend a week in Corsica, soaking up the sun and generally spoiling herself.

The notaires were on Rue Republique not far from Montmartre and she was received by a very charming M Albert Condom. A surname which she at first thought she had misheard until he presented his card.

'Ah Madame Philips, please take a seat. Would you like some coffee?' He seemed to take her nod as an affirmative as he poured out a small portion of black coffee from a *cafetiere.*

'Your English is very good, Monsieur er... Condom.' Julia blushed as she realised she had hesitated over his name, but if he had noticed, M. Condom was a perfect diplomat.

'I spent a year in London, when I left the Lycee working for the travel company Cooks. It was my father's idea and it worked brilliantly, not only did I polish my English, but I got to travel back to the sun!'

'You put me to shame.' replied Julia, 'my French is poor, but I do try, as I think it is such bad manners not to attempt to understand the language of the country you are visiting, even if you are an embarrassment!'

'Please do not worry, I am sure that your attempts are very, how shall I say, *diplomatique!'*

Julia smiled and regarded him over her coffee. About forty something years of age, she guessed, just beginning to go grey, quite distinguished really. She imagined he had a chic wife and three children, living in the suburbs, probably within cycling distance, after all he was quite slim. His wife would wait for him each evening with an aperitif before sitting down to dinner. Or, he could have tragically lost his wife and now lived for his work, which he took home and only escaped when he went to his local restaurant most evenings for dinner.

'Madame Phillips... Madame Phillips!'

Julia came to with a start. 'Sorry, I was day dreaming.'

'As I was trying to say, with regard to your uncle M. Henry Wilberforce.'

'Sorry, please do carry on!' Julia felt her cheeks hot with embarrassment.

'Thank you.' M. Condom smiled

Julia thought he looked quite attractive when he smiled.

'Now as I was saying. Your Uncle Henry. He came to us about ten years ago. At the time he had bought a property in Antibes ...'

'I know.' interrupted Julia enthusiastically, ' I spent a week there some ten years ago when... oh sorry!'

'Oui... in Antibes. Now at the time M Wilberforce asked me to send a codicil to his English lawyers.'

'What is a codicil?'

'In England it is an addition or amendment to a will.'

'Ah!' Julia nodded.

M Condom sighed and continued, 'In the codicil he made an amendment to his will stating that he left his house in Antibes to his daughter, Lucille, to be held in trust by yourself until she is twenty one. In return you may reside or stay there for any time in a calendar year, excluding the month of August when it may be used exclusively by Lucille and her mother, Mahilia.' He paused and took a sip of his coffee. 'However, there is one stipulation. In the event of Mahilia dying before her daughter reaches the age of twenty one, you must agree to act as her guardian.' Seeing the look on

Julia's face he added quickly, 'the mother has agreed and I have the papers already signed.'

Julia stared at M Condom, opened her mouth as if to speak but closed it again quickly. There was a minute or so of silence and the notaire as if embarrassed said quite quickly 'Of course there will be expenses and your Uncle has left you a generous sum to maintain the property and for your personal use, nearly one million euro.'

Shocked, Julia repeated 'One million Euro!'

'I am of course only referring to his assets in France and not to his English estate.'

'Er, when does this start.' Julia began to take it all on board. 'I mean… when do I have to say 'Yes'?'

'Well, shall we say that you will let me know in a week or so. I would like to settle the estate. In the meantime we will arrange for the property to be inspected and a report sent to you, together with all the papers.'

Julia stood up and heard her reply in a rather dazed voice. 'Fine I will call you in a week, probably after I have seen your report.'

It was ten days later that the postman called bearing a large packet with a French stamp. Carrying it through to what she called her study in the alcove off the living room, Julia spent an hour wading through the papers. After which she got up, made a mug of coffee and carried it out into the garden. She was still shaken, not only by the fact that she was now a wealthy woman, but that she had inherited a bizarre situation.

But it was a very serious woman that sat on a garden bench opposite the statute of Aphrodite on that lovely sunny morning talking to herself. 'So you see, here I am stuck with managing a whopping villa in France - for what? Maybe a holiday now and then, but in ten years it disappears. It seems I don't even get the pleasure of meeting Uncle Henry's amour or his offspring.' Julia suddenly sat up. 'My God, she's my cousin!'

'Who's your cousin?' came a voice from the front gate.

'Tom! Come in and have some coffee.' Julia jumped up and greeted her neighbour.

'What's this about a cousin?'

Julia led Tom back into the kitchen and made some more coffee. Sitting again in the garden she filled in the story line. 'So you see I am in the strange position of a guardian in waiting.'

'Do you want to be her guardian?'

'I don't know. After all, she lives in France and if anything happens to her mother I doubt if she would want to leave her native country.'

Tom nodded. 'Well I suggest you stop worrying, accept the legacy and until and only if, something happens to her mother, take it from there. Think of the painting opportunities you will have in Antibes!'

Julia smiled. 'True,' she paused and added wistfully, 'I can't help thinking the whole scenario could be the making of a splendid novel!'

Julia and the Village Fete

If there is any event, in a village, that brings out the best and the worst in people, then it must be the Village Fete.

When art teacher, Julia Philips, moved into the village of Upper Monksford some eighteen months ago, she vowed never to involve herself in any village activity, other than as a friendly supporter. That vow was broken within seventy-eight days of her arrival!

Her first foray into village life was when she was co-opted into painting the backdrop for the village school nativity play. At least she had an assistant in the form of Marcus, aged seven, who insisted they included a dinosaur in the stable. Which was not quite as bad as six year old Katie's contribution of a baby doll. This turned out to be a look-a-like of Pamela Anderson, from *Bay Watch;* much to the interest of the older boys.

Then two months later Julia was a stand-in guest speaker, to the Young Wives Club. A little confusing as, in the front row at the village hall sat Old Mrs Hubbard who was at least eighty-four; whilst in the back row, sat Sharon House, aged eighteen, very pregnant and not yet married.

There followed a lull over the Easter period, until a phone call from a very persuasive Vicar cajoled Julia into attending a meeting of that year's Village Fete committee.

The Vicar, Archie Thursfield, opened the meeting and praised last year's success, particularly in obtaining the local TV weather girl, who opened the Fete to a record crowd.

'So, has anybody got any ideas for this year's Opener?'

Silence reigned as he surveyed the blank look on all their faces. 'Come along, surely someone has a celebrity tucked away somewhere?'

The silence continued until old Mrs Lemmings, who always ran the white elephant stall, piped up. 'How about you, Vicar?'

He shook his head and smiled. 'We need to attract visitors and for some villagers I haven't the right charisma!' Julia coughed politely and the Vicar glanced over towards her. 'Ah, Julia, fresh to the scene, with fresh ideas?'

'It just occurred to me,' Julia paused with embarrassment 'the date of the Fete is Saturday, July the fourth.'

'Yes?' The Vicar replied.

'It's American Independence Day. How about getting an American to open it!'

There was a moment when she thought there were mutterings of discontent, but Archie Thursfield interrupted them and beamed at Julia.

'Good idea. But who?'

'Well there is an American Museum not far away. How about asking the curator?' Heads nodded and Julia, encouraged, offered to approach them. Before she knew it, the village had picked her up and swept her along on the tide. She was now firmly ensconced in village life.

Julia had great success with the request and the Assistant Curator, who was a Professor of American Folk Lore accepted with wild enthusiasm. This was noted in the minutes of the next meeting of the Village Fete committee and promptly forgotten until four days before the event, when Julia bumped into the Vicar in the village post office.

'Good morning, Archie. It looks as if we shall have a good day for the Fete.'

'Hello, Julia. I hope so. Tell me have you contacted the speaker again?'

'No, but I will give them a ring, when I get home.' Julia gave herself a mental slap on the wrist for not doing it beforehand. They exchanged further pleasantries before parting and Julia, having made her purchases, walked the short distance to her cottage.

'Hello, is that the American Museum?' Julia put the phone on speaker as she fished out the relevant notes from a wallet file. 'Yes, I need to speak to Joy McKnair, please.... sorry my name is Julia Philips from Upper Monksford. Miss McKnair is opening our Village Fete this weekend.' There was a long pause as the person on the other end of the call explained to Julia that Miss McKnair was no longer in the country as her visa had expired and she had been effectively deported!

Julia put the phone down with exaggerated care and swore. 'Bugger! Now what do I do?' She sat and looked at the phone for several seconds and then picked it up and dialled a number.

'Ann, it's Julia .... Fine, actually no, I'm not fine I have a major crisis on my hands ... Well you know we have the village fete this coming weekend ... it was my job to get an American to open it, I managed to get a curator of the American Museum to agree, but it appears she has been deported!'

There was a pause as Ann made muffled noises down the phone. 'Yes, but what do I do?' wailed Julia. 'It would be nice if we had a tame American ... No, the Head Curator is off on a course and all the other staff there are English.' There was a silence as Ann spoke to her husband. Then with a little sigh of relief, Julia listened optimistically to Ann's reply, thanked her, before turning off her phone.

Upper Monksford had a splendid Elizabethan manor and every year, dear old Sir Harry Berwick opened the grounds to the village; the residents in return set up a variety of stalls on his immaculate lawns; bowled skittles for a pig, threw hoops for prizes, or just sat and enjoyed cream teas. Sir Harry would stroll from the White Elephant stall to the Bathroom stall and on to the Sweet stall followed by the Bottle stall. Here he would adjust his monocle before lecturing the stallholder not to allow young Marcus to claim the bottle of whisky, the boy had just won. At each stall he would take out his wallet and present the stallholder with a crisp new five pound note, by way of a donation. Never would he actually buy anything or participate.

The day dawned bright and warm. The Vicar accosted Julia, who was in the process of helping old Mrs Lemmings on the White Elephant stall. He stood ringing his hands and looked worried

'Ah, Julia, now you are confident that this er ... American professor of history will be here?'

Julia smiled and nodded. 'All is well, Archie!'

'I know I shouldn't doubt you, but it was quite a

shock. Still if the worst comes to the worst, I'll say a few words.'

Fifteen minutes before the fete was due to open, the young car park attendant, seconded for the day, goggled at the sight of a luxury coach pulling in to the manor drive. Julia hurried forward in time to meet a tall youngish looking man leading a party off the vehicle.

She held out her hand in greeting. 'Good afternoon, My name is Julia Roberts and you must be with Professor Pritchard's party.'

The young man shook her hand and smiled. 'No. I am the Professor!'

'Oh! I'm sorry I was expecting an older man. And my friend, Ann said you would be bringing just a few friends!' She gazed in astonishment as the coach disgorged around forty people.

'Is there a problem?' The Professor lifted both his hands as if to apologise.

'Oh no! Certainly not. The Vicar will be delighted.' Julia led the way through the entrance to the Fete, explaining en route, that they would meet the Lord and Lady of the Manor and then she would introduce them to the public, when he could declare the fete open.

Julia led the Professor over to meet Sir Harry and Lady Berwick. Lady Berwick seemed delighted that the young good looking professor bent to kiss her on both cheeks and insisted on kissing him back!.. So much so that Julia and the Vicar quickly ushered the professor to the microphone.

Sir Harry, who was a good deal older than his wife, at first looked taken aback by this public display of affection, began to tut-tut. But it was when the professor, in opening the Fete, expressed his own thanks for the invitation, that Sir Harry's face began to turn a deeper shade of red. The professor started by calling up the visiting Americans, who trooped up the steps of the terrace. It was an incongruous sight, with Bermuda shorts and tee shirts bearing wild messages, emerging from the very English crowd of summer dresses and chinos and check shirts.

They stood on the terrace steps, facing the puzzled faces of the villagers, and with hands across their hearts, they performed a rendering of My America. This was the last straw for Sir Harry; his beloved English countryside turned into a version of the musical Carousel. His face turned a deep purple and spluttering he was led away, not to be seen again that day.

Very much later, the visitors from across the "pond", well watered and fed on tea and scones, followed by strawberries and cream, declared it the best day of their tour. One old lady who was visiting with her twenty year old grand daughter had bought mementos for all her family. She clutched a bag of Victorian bottles from the White Elephant stall, all dug up in Mrs Lemming's garden by the indomitable George.

Later that afternoon the professor mysteriously vanished. It was discovered subsequently that he was given a very personal and private tour of the manor by Lady Florence.

At the end of the fete, the Vicar gathered all the organisers and helpers together and after congratulating them, produced a small bundle of crsip new five pound notes. 'With Lady Berwicks's thanks' he announced with a knowing smile.

Julia and the locked door mystery

Julia wove her way through the mature students hard at work in her art class. Past green cows with bright orange udders and John's eighth attempt at the Mona Lisa, finally pausing behind one of her students, whose painting she immediately recognised.

'Isn't that Dolly's farm shop on the Pencastle road?'

'Mm...' murmured Ann, 'Something I have been meaning to have a stab at for ages. I just love the colour of the random stone they used to build the barn.'

'I agree, it is an exceptionally deep coloured sandstone.'

'I think they quarried it at the back of the farm, probably a couple of centuries ago.' Ann wiped her brush on a rag and leant back on her stool.

'That reminds me,' Julia added. 'Can you and Mike come to lunch next Sunday week?'

Before Ann could reply they were interrupted by Brian, a rather noisy class member who, with his arms full of canvases, was trying to open a cupboard door by banging it with his foot.

'Oh God, Brian is at it again. Give me a ring, Ann.' Saying which, she wove her way back across the room to confront Brian.

'Brian, what are you trying to do?'

'Sorry about that, ' he countered cheerfully 'Just trying to open the cupboard door.'

'I think it would be easier if you used your hands!' Julia replied with a little sarcasm and duly undid the door for him.

Smiling to herself Julia went back to her students, stopping to enquire from the artist with the green cow and bright orange udders why there appeared to be only two teats.

The artist regarded her tutor and sarcastically replied, 'Balls... It's a bull!'

'Julia, this roast beef is delicious!'

Julia smiled at her luncheon guests. 'Thank you. I'm a firm believer in supporting the local farms and...' she paused and looked across the table to Ann, 'it's from Dolly's farm shop. The one in your painting.'

'Good move,' replied Anne's husband, Mike. 'Here's to the cook,' and lifted his wine glass.

The fourth member of the party, Tom, Julia's neighbour, lifted his glass in unison.

Julia acknowledged the toast and then leant forward in a confidential manner. 'Actually, it seems Dolly has a problem. She told me that for the past few weeks she has been losing small amounts of stock. Some fruit here and veggies there. But they cannot work out who or how it is being stolen. Probably up your street, Tom!'

Tom, the retired police inspector, carefully set down his knife and fork. 'Have they got CCTV?'

'No. Dolly says it's too expensive.'

'Staff?'

'There's only Dolly and young Lucy. She's just sixteen and pretty naïve. Perhaps you could have a look for them, Tom?'

'I'm not sure about that. They should contact their neighbourhood Policeman. I wouldn't like to put his or her nose out of joint.'

-

Julia had forgotten all about their lunchtime conversation until the following Friday when she was helping out at a curry evening in the village hall, organised by the local branch of the WI , to raise funds for a school in Africa.

Looking up from serving another portion of chicken tikka she found the outstretched hand of Tom holding forth a plate.

'Smells good!' he grinned.

'Tom! I didn't rate you as a WI supporter. Unless you are volunteering for their next calendar!' She giggled.

'Well I thought I would support a good cause.'

'Well keep a seat for me. I will join you as soon as soon as I can.'

Five minutes later Julia tucked into her curry as Tom leant back with a contented sigh.

'Have some local brew.' Tom leant across and topped up Julia's glass with a light beer that gave forth a delightful aroma of malted barley and hops.

'Very good!' murmured Julia, having tasted the beer. She picked up the beer bottle and read the label - *Maiden's Blush - a young tempting brew.*' Hmm, where have you been shopping?'

'Dolly's Farm Shop! It's a local brew and according to Dolly another one of the disappearing stock items.'

'So it's still going on?'

'It seems so.' He explained that the police were baffled and had said they could do no more than suggest she changes the locks. But it appears her husband put a new Yale lock on last month. 'I agreed to go up there tomorrow morning. Would you like to come?'

'Mm...' Julia finished a mouthful of curry. 'But I don't think I would be very good at detective work.'

Tom smiled. 'Two heads are better than one.'

And so it was, the next morning Tom drove Julia out to Dolly's Farm Shop. Julia had never assisted on a crime scene before, even one as trivial as this and she dutifully followed Tom as he toured the building, examining all the windows and the front and side entrances. He even checked the ceilings and floors, the latter of which consisted of solid concrete, but she made no comment, merely taking in all Tom said.

At last they finished and Tom insisted on buying coffee and flapjacks which they took out to a table on the patio and sat in the pale October sunshine.

'Well what do you think?' asked Tom.

'Very nice!' replied Julia with a mouthful of flapjack.

'Not the flapjacks!'

'Both!' as she took a sip of coffee.

'Julia! As an acting detective constable you are very obtuse!'

Tom's companion smiled sweetly. 'Well guv, it could be an inside job!'

'I agree, it could be if there were an 'inside' - apart from Dolly and her husband, George, we just have young Lucy.'

'I somehow don't rate her.'

'Then someone has a key and gets in after hours.'

Tom shook his head. 'The front double doors are locked and bolted from the inside and the side door is self locking with the new Yale lock when anyone leaves. The windows are barred, the ceiling and floors all solid.'

'What about deliveries?'

'Good thought. But they all go to the side door and ring a bell. There is a kind of goods inwards and they get checked by Dolly. The delivery people never go in the shop.'

They mused over the conundrum for sometime before making their adieus, agreeing to return if they thought of anything.

On the Sunday, Julia had promised to visit Ann, who lived in a nearby village, and they ended up by taking her dogs for a walk on the common. It was whilst they were making their way through the adjoining woods that her friend tutted and picked up an empty beer bottle.

'Just look at that. If it breaks, some poor animal will cut itself and probably bleed to death.' With a delicate flourish she dropped the bottle in a rubbish bin, which was quite close by.

'Hold on a minute. What was the label on the bottle?' Julia asked peering into the bin.

'I couldn't care less - it just makes my blood boil,' retorted Anne.

Julia found a stick and poked around in the rubbish. 'I thought so, Maiden's Blush. It's the same brand that is disappearing from Dolly's Farm Shop.'

'Oh really.'

'Mm... I wonder who got rid of that up here?'

'Probably one of those lads who hang around on the common.'

Julia thought for a moment or two and then

asked. 'Do they ever have any girls with them?'

'Possibly. I thought I saw that pretty young blonde girl Lucy in Pencastle with one of the boys you see up here. Colin - a bit of a tearaway. A loud mouth. He reminds me of Brian in the art class, but not so intelligent.'

It was a pensive Julia who drove home that afternoon and after going into her house for a few minutes she drove on to Tom's cottage and rang the bell.

'This is an unexpected pleasure,' Tom greeted her as he opened the door and held it wide. 'Come in.'

'Actually Tom I have an idea. Can we go out to Dollys?'

Tom looked at his watch. 'Well they will be closing in half an hour.'

'All the better. Come on and bring your deerstalker or what ever it is you detectives wear!'

Dolly was on her own and about to close up when they arrived. Julia explained that she thought that she may have solved the case of the locked door and, although she wouldn't bet on it, the person responsible.

With Dolly's agreement the two of them settled down in the stock room with a cup of tea and some more flapjacks, as Julia said it could be a long wait. But she took Dolly's private number and promised to call if they had had enough or were successful.

'Well are you going to explain?' asked Tom not without a little irritation.

'Well it was Anne who gave me the idea and the link to the possible culprit.'

'So how was it done?'

'Wait and see - but expect a noise from the shop to warn us.'

For the umpteenth time Julia looked at her mobile phone and sighed. They had stopped playing cards and she was half dozing when they heard a couple of bangs from the front of the shop. Tom held up his hand.

'That's it!' He looked quizzically at Julia. She nodded. 'Right I'll go out of the side door and give me one minute and I will follow him or her in. You go through into the shop and throw on all the lights. The switch is inside the door as Dolly showed us.'

One minute later she did as she was told and found herself behind a startled youth aged about sixteen. He turned and was confronted by a six foot two ex policeman. His shoulders drooped and his face looked startled as Julia said to Tom. 'Let me introduce you to Lucy's boyfriend, Colin.'

The shock of being caught deflated Colin, and he was led into the back room. When Dolly arrived she insisted on ringing the police (her crime tolerance was zero). As she explained 'I worked hard to get this going and no towrag is going to get away with it.'

Privately Julia guessed that the courts would be lenient but she agreed with Dolly and they felt little pity for young Colin as he was driven away.

'There's just one thing,' Tom said to Julia.

'Yes?' replied Julia innocently.

'OK. Accepting that you found out about the link to Lucy, and it was lucky he chose tonight to come back - but how the hell did he get in and then lock the door behind him?'

Julia crooked her finger and they followed her to the open doors where she pointed to the Yale lock which was still in the engaged position. She bolted the other door at the top and then waiving them all outside pulled the other door to until the latch clicked into place.

'You see only one door is bolted, but it holds the other one with the lock. However if you thump it hard on the outside of the bolt it falls down and the doors which aren't absolutely flush, just push open! Then he did what I have just done and in the morning you unlock in the normal way.'

'Hmm,' grunted Tom 'It wouldn't have worked with a lock on the bottom. Or if the bolt knob had been turned to the side. Or if the doors and been a better fit!'

'True, but Dolly wasn't to know that.'

Dolly laughed, 'That's right dear, but what made you think of it?'

Julia smiled. 'A belligerent young man in my art class who always kicked a cupboard door to open it!'

'Do you think Lucy knew what was going on?' asked Dolly sadly.

'I doubt it.' replied Julia with equal sadness.

Julia and *The Rifleman*

The auctioneers, Johnson & Johnson of Pencastle, were having their monthly art sale and Julia Philips decided it was worth a visit. As an art teacher she had acquired an eye for nice pieces and kept a close watch on the local salerooms. Several local artist's work from the 19th and 20th centuries were on offer this month and she had seen a watercolour she liked, at the preview. The auction had only just started when Julia and her friend Diana arrived at the sale rooms.

'What lot number are you bidding for?' Diana gazed around the vast emporium that housed the sale.

'Oh it's not 'til Lot 397. Probably this afternoon. Look it's over here.' She weaved her way amongst laden tables to the far wall which had around sixty pictures haphazardly hung along the length of the room.

'Do you mean this one?'

Julia moved over to where Diana was standing in front of a rather dark watercolour. 'Mm ... Do you like it?'

'Not really. It's dirty and to be truthful, a bit gloomy! What on earth attracted you to this picture?'

'Well, it's dated at 1814 and is reputed to be a recruiting party arriving outside an inn,' Julia replied. 'In a way it reminds me of our local, The Stags Head.'

They stood in front of the picture for a few seconds. 'Mm ... you may be right. It does look like the village green, although I don't remember the pond.'

'No, maybe it went at the end of the last century. But I just like the picture. It captures the light on the stonework, even before the picture is cleaned.' Julia smiled. 'I just like it!'

'Okay. Unless you want to watch the auction, I'll treat you to a snack lunch at Pan's Coffee House.'

'You're on!'

Duncan Roberts sat at his cluttered desk in what he called his office. In truth it was a sparsely furnished box room, next door to their living room, on the first floor of The Stags Head.

He shifted in his chair and shivered, despite the fact it was a balmy day in early summer. He turned as if half expecting to find Vickie, his wife, looking over his shoulder. She had never liked this room since she swore she saw a form standing next to the stone fireplace. Duncan had laughed at her fears and gladly taken on the room as his office.

His reverie was disturbed by his wife, who was calling from the bottom of the stairs. Making his way down the broad oak staircase he found Vickie waiting for him.

'Darling, we need some more Medoc from the cellar and could you change the G G Best Bitter?'

'No problem. How many and which year?'

'Oh, four should be enough of the '05.'

Duncan made his way down into the cellar. It had been renovated back in the sixties and although the beer pumps and pipes were modern, they had left the original stone shelves where the wine racks were. Having dealt with the beer, Duncan made his way over to where the wines were stored. At the end of one row he moved a wooden panel that he used to shield the better wines. The panel was at least five foot by three feet and very heavy. Duncan swore as he dropped it on to his toe. 'I must get rid of this, sometime!' he muttered to himself. Still muttering he struggled up the stairs with a basket containing the required wine.

It was a good fortnight later when Julia was invited, by her neighbour Tom Ryder, to lunch at The Stags Head. Vickie Roberts had greeted them at the entrance to the restaurant and shown them to their table.

Still standing Julia said, 'I'll be back in a minute.'

'Fine, shall I order some wine?' Taking Julia's nod as an affirmative he sat studying the wine list and then the menu. It was quite some five minutes before she returned. 'Ah there you are. I thought you may have changed your mind about lunch.' He poured out a glass of wine for her.

Julia smiled. 'Thanks. Sorry about that. I was just reading an old cutting hanging on the wall in the hall.'

They had an excellent lunch and complimented Vickie when she came to offer them coffee.

'Thank you. It's a pity we can't get more business. Duncan is very worried about the lack of trade in the pub.'

Julia stirred her coffee and looking up said, 'Perhaps what you need is a gimmick. How about your ghost that's supposed to haunt the place?'

'The previous owners made a song and dance about it. But I don't think you should laugh at such things. Now if you'll excuse me.' Vickie answered sharply and made her way back to the kitchen door.

'I didn't mean to upset the woman.' Julia frowned.

'What do you know about a ghost?' Tom asked with some curiosity.

'Because there is a framed newspaper cutting hanging on the wall in the hall. However, it's a strange coincidence, but I happened to buy a water colour last month and having done a bit of research I think that it is this inn. Although the name has changed, it is reputed that it's haunted. Look, Duncan has just come into the dining room, let's ask him!'

Duncan hesitated. 'Vickie is very wary of talking about the Lady in Grey. She believes the story is true!'

It was a week later when Julia went back to The Stags Head. She was carrying the watercolour she had purchased in Pencastle. Duncan Roberts met her in the reception hall of the inn.

'Hello, Julia. Your phone call had us intrigued. Come up to our sitting room, Vickie is getting us some coffee.'

She followed him through the reception and up the broad staircase. Duncan stopped outside an open door and ushered Julia through. Their sitting room was large and comfortable with the stone fireplace filled by a huge vase of tall yellow gladioli.

'As promised I've brought the watercolour to show you.' Julia pulled the picture from the bag she had carried them in.

'Good Lord!' exclaimed Duncan as she laid them on his desk. 'This is our inn!' Duncan picked up the picture and peered at it closely.

'That's what set me thinking ...' Julia's reply was interrupted by Vickie coming in and carrying a tray of coffee and biscuits.

'Hallo, Julia. I'm sorry to keep you waiting, but I was just briefing chef on today's menus.'

'Vickie, do look. Julia has brought over an early watercolour of The Stags Head '

Julie put down the tray she had been carrying and picked up the picture. 'Well it does look like our place. But we don't have a pond by the green.'

'No. Old George was telling me that it was filled in by a local farmer during the Second World War. Some bright Herbert of an Air Raid Warden reckoned it shone too brightly in the moonlight and after one or two raids they filled it in!'

'When do you think it was painted?' asked Vicky.

'Now we come to the first point. If you look carefully at the sign you will see that it is not The Stags Head. The man, I am reliably informed, is a Rifleman. In my research I found that the inn was known as The Rifleman from 1799 when one Tom King, the eldest son of the landlord joined the 95th Rifles. In your cutting from the Pencastle Times it mentions The Lady in Grey, the ghost that is supposed to haunt this inn. According to the article, her son was Sergeant Tom King of the 95th Rifles and he was reported lost, presumed killed at the battle of Talavera in 1809. His mother, known as The Lady in Grey was supposed to have died of a broken heart. '

Duncan jumped up. 'We have the painting. It was in this room when we came, but Julia felt uneasy with it, so it now hangs in my study. Stay there I'll get it.' He crossed the room and left by a small door on the far side. Returning a few seconds later he carried the small oil painting over to Julia.

'It's beautiful!' she exclaimed. 'Why don't you

like it, Vickie?'

'I don't know. It was hanging here in the room when we came and there is a request by all the past landlords that it must always remain here. The story is she is still waiting for her son to come home.' She lowered her voice and added. 'I asked Duncan to move it ... you see I have seen the Lady in Grey!'

'Really! Where exactly? '

'In the office.'

'Mm ... I can well understand it. But, that brings me to my second point. Examine the watercolour I purchased. In particular the woman in the doorway - here I brought a magnifying glass.' Julia held it up for Vickie.

Peering through the glass, Vickie suddenly whispered. 'The Lady in Grey!'

Duncan took the glass from his wife and examined the picture. 'Good God, I think you're right!'

'Now study the soldiers and tell me what you see,' Julia instructed Duncan.

'Well ... they're soldiers! No, wait! I think they may be riflemen. They have a green uniform and the man in the front looks like a sergeant, he has stripes.'

'Full marks!' exclaimed Julia. 'You see, I think this is Sergeant Tom King!'

'Good Lord! Can you be sure?' Duncan straightened up.

'Not absolutely, but the odd thing is the date by the signature, 1814. If it was Tom King, he was supposed to have died at Talavera in 1809! We could find out from the military archives.'

Vickie peered once again at the picture. 'She

looks as if she is waving to one of the soldiers. As you said, it could be her son. He's come home!'

Julia smiled. 'A nice idea. Thinking about it, I would like to give you the picture to hang in the dining room downstairs.'

'We cannot accept that!' Duncan replied.

'No, especially as you have just bought it,' added Vickie. 'No, if you insist on us having it, we must pay for it.'

'Absolutely!' agreed her husband.

'Well, if you insist,' agreed Julia. 'But only on the condition that it hangs in the inn's dining room. If it is okay with you, may I accept payment in kind, in the form of a few meals? The painting was less than two hundred pounds.'

'Agreed!' the Roberts chorused.

It must have been at least four weeks later when Julia decided to return Tom's luncheon treat with an invitation to dinner at The Stags Head. At the end of their meal, Duncan asked if he and Vickie could join them.

'I must say you seem to have had nearly a house full to-night.' Tom said to them both as they sat down.

'I know. Its so heartening,' smiled Vickie. 'But, better than that, Duncan has some really exciting news for you.'

The two guests regarded Duncan who had a broad smile across his face. 'We owe you more than a meal or two. Firstly we had a visit from the curator of the Riflemen's' museum. Tom King was discharged in 1814, so that is, in all probability, him in the picture you see hanging above you.' He paused dramatically. 'But, in addition, when I was turning out the cellar, which I had been meaning to do since we arrived, I made the most extraordinary find. It seems when they changed the name of the inn again, around 1900, someone put the old Rifleman sign in the cellar.'

'You mean the rifleman as shown in the painting!' exclaimed Julia, excitedly.

'Exactly. We contacted the brewery and they were so interested we had two directors and an art expert down to see it. We have one of the only original 18th century signs still in existence. Technically it is ours, as we purchased all the loose fixtures and fittings. We are now told it is worth around sixty thousand pounds on the open market!'

'Wow! What a find. Can we see it?' asked Julia.

Duncan shook his head. 'We have sent it up for auction, but here is a photo of the board and ... here is a letter from the Managing Director of the brewery asking us if we would consider changing the name of the inn back to The Rifleman.'

'Will you?' Julia asked bluntly.

Duncan shook his head again. 'I don't think so. Not only do we have to think of our customers and the locals, but it has been The Stags Head for around 100 years.'

'Let's hope the Lady in Grey agrees.' murmured Julia. They all turned and stared at her.

Julia and the good deed

Julia did not see herself as a Samaritan, although to be fair she was always there if a friend ever shouted for help.
So when Celia rang and asked if she could come and stay for a few days as things were not too good at home she acquiesced with good grace and welcomed her with a warm hug.
After a couple of days, in which the tissues were all used up and the new gin bottle got to the point of recycling, Julia was feeling a little fraught herself. Especially as the day was Wednesday and that was the day of her art class in Pencastle.
'I would love to come,' announced Celia. 'Its ages since I lifted a brush, that is if you don't mind...'
What could she say? Julia smiled graciously and then a thought struck her. 'Lord, I haven't got a subject matter for tonight!'
'Don't worry.' enthused Celia 'Let's do a still life with some flowers from your garden. Let me go and pick a bunch and you can arrange it when we get there.'
'Well... I do have to go and do some shopping and that would be a great help.' Besides replacing the gin and the odd bottle of wine they were getting a bit low on food. Julia made a mental note to ask Celia how long her absence from George was likely to be.
Wednesday night in late July was always a bit of a lottery, mainly because the school holidays had just begun and those members attending would usually be

the ones without children to worry about. Celia had rung George in the day to find out how he was coping. They had two children at boarding school and they were due home that weekend. George must have been pleading on bended knees as there were some conciliatory noises that Julia could not help overhearing, followed by an announcement from Celia that her husband was coming down to pick her up on Sunday morning.

As it turned out, the attendance at art class that evening was above average and before they all arrived Julia had set to and arranged a simple vase of poppies and cereals, such as the green and golden corn and barley stalks Celia had collected that afternoon. She stepped back to admire the still life when a voice close to her ear made her jump.

'Ah, the simple things in life!'

Dryden was, in her eyes, a spoilt young man whose mother indulged him in anything he asked for. Having spent a year in Paris he was now back living with his mother in the next village. Julia had met the lady in question, Dorothy Marchbanks, and had felt small sympathy with the woman. Her husband had long given up trying to control Dorothy spoiling her only child. In Dorothy's eyes, her son was about to be recognised as the reincarnation of Degas - whereas it was very far from the truth.

Julia moved to one side and regarded him closely. 'I trust we haven't been indulging!' she admonished him light heartedly.

'Miss Philips, how can you say such a thing?' Dryden dramatically flicked back his shoulder length hair.

'Quite easily. You forget, I know your parents.'

'True. But as an artist I feel no constraints.'

Containing herself with what she thought was remarkable composure Julia made a final adjustment to the arrangement and then stepped back to clap her hands. 'Can you all take your seats, please? Anne, you need to move a little closer and Mr Harding can you move your easel a little to the left? Thank you.'

The class settled down to draw, some in charcoal and some in pastels, but most were using watercolours. It was this medium that her friend had chosen to use and Julia was quite surprised with her progress.

'Celia! That's very good.'

'Thank you, Julia. It's wonderful to feel I haven't lost my touch.'

'Why did you stop?'

'Oh you know - children - gardening - dogs - moving house - hamsters - housework and husband!'

Julia smiled and patted her shoulder. 'Keep it up - it's good therapy. By the way I saw young Dryden talking to you rather intensely just now. What was he asking you?'

'Oh nothing dear, we were talking about the arrangement. I told him I had chosen them and picked them for you.'

'Really! That's all?'

'That's all.'

'Mm…' Julia moved on with a puzzled look on her face. She had strong reservations about Dryden!

The evening went well and there were some good results and, Julia had to admit, some not so good results. She blamed herself; charcoal pencils were OK for a quick sketch but you need delicacy and colour.

Julia resolved to be firmer in future. Celia chatted away on the way home and she soon forgot about the disappointments and bathed in her friend's enthusiasm. It was on Friday afternoon when returning from another shopping trip, admittedly with not so much alcohol this time, that Julia thought she saw Dryden cycling off down the lane away from her house. Laden with plastic shopping bags she entered the kitchen to find a flushed looking Celia.

'Ah... Julia, you're back!'

'Yes. It's me.' Julia narrowed her eyes as if trying to see something in Celia's demeanour. 'Er... did I see Dryden just leaving?' she asked innocently.

'Dryden?'

Julia could have sworn Celia blushed.

'Oh, do you mean the boy at the art class.'

'That's right! Dryden!'

'You saw him?'

'Yes... he was pedalling away when I pulled up.'

'Ah... a pity, he called to see you.'

'He did see me. He just rode off!'

'Ah... perhaps he changed his mind. Now if you'll excuse me I think I'll change my dress for something cooler.' Celia made a bee line for the door and shut it firmly behind her.

Julia stood for a second as if in thought and then aloud said. 'Dryden? ... Celia? ... ' She shook her head. 'No it can't be!'

They spent a quiet evening, most of it in the cool garden shade; having eaten al fresco, they enjoyed the long summer evening reading interspersed with smatterings of conversation. Julia wasn't sure whether her friend was avoiding conversation or whether she was beginning to relax.

Saturday was another hot day and Julia was irritated to find she needed more vegetables.

'Do you need anything, Celia? I forgot the vegetables and you must stay for Sunday lunch before you go back.'

Celia smiled wanly and then mumbled about getting Richard to see some sense and see things her way for a change. 'Anyone would think I was having an affair,' she added bitterly.

Julia shook her head. It was no business of hers what Celia was up to. At the village shop she ran into Tom Ryder, a retired police inspector, he was the instigator of their Neighbourhood Watch.

'Hallo Tom, how's crime?'

'Ah Julia. How are you? I haven't seen you around recently.'

'Oh I'm around alright! But just not in circulation! I'm doing my Good Samaritan bit!'

'Well done, but when you have saved whoever it is, come and have lunch with me.'

'I'd love to.'

'Well I must be away - having a meeting with the local headmaster - you know the usual stuff.'

Julia didn't know what the usual stuff was, but nodded understandingly.

Back at the cottage she joined Celia in the garden. Her borders were alive with insects and butterflies; pollen laden bees were adding their presence to the harmony. As Julia's eyes wandered along the borders they stopped, unsure what she had missed but fully aware that something had changed. She suddenly leant forward and putting down her glass of wine she exclaimed. 'Poppies!'

Celia lowered her book. 'Pardon, dear!'
'I said poppies!'
'That's what I thought you said!'
'I mean where are they?'
'Well along the end of that bed… ' Her voice trailed off as she stared across the garden. 'They were there on Wednesday…right opposite that statute.'
'Yes, Aphrodite. How many did you pick?' She stood up and slowly made her way down the garden.
'Well… only about five heads,' Celia's voice rose an octave or two, 'but there were dozens of blooms, I don't understand it.' She followed her friend to the point were the plants stood minus their heads.
'Nor do I. Something or someone has cut them off!'
'Well it wasn't me!'
'I didn't think it was, but who or what would steal all my lovely flowers?'
'Perhaps it was an animal!'
'Celia, I hardly think an Ayrshire cow or a Gloucester Old Spot pig popped in for a quick snack.'

Later that afternoon Tom rang and invited Julia over for drinks.
'Sorry Tom, I have a friend staying at the moment.'
'Bring them over. Is it a he or a she?'
'She. Celia is having a break from her family.'
'Good. Bring her over, she will probably need to escape her Samaritan for a while!'
'Tom Ryder, you're incorrigible. We'll be over at six.'

Trapped up against Tom's patio doors, Julia peered over old Mr Peterson's shoulder and smiled.

Tom had steered Celia away from the other guests and sat her down at a garden table. The two were having a serious discussion. Trying desperately not to appear rude, Julia excused herself from the exciting topic of new loos for the village hall and made her way through the other guests who were standing on the patio sipping drinks and more than likely debating the colour schemes for the said new loos. She made her way over the lawn to the couple who looked up as she approached.

'Julia, your friend has been very helpful. Not only has she solved my problem but probably yours as well!'

'I didn't know I had a problem!'

'Supplying raw materials to manufacture a Class A drug, for example?'

'What?'

'Your young friend Dryden went back to school this week. Only it wasn't a reunion. Apparently he has been using the school laboratory to manufacture opium.'

'Oh my god - the poppies.' Julia held her hand over her mouth.

'Right in one. Poor Celia fell for his young charms and whilst she was getting him coffee he did some gardening. When we met this evening I told her of our drug talks to the school and in particular of the break-in last night, where someone had used the school chemistry lab to try and produce opium. It was when I mentioned the discarded poppy heads to your friend here that she told her story.'

'Oh Julia I hope I did the right thing,' Celia said anxiously. 'I mean I know you know his parents.'

'You were quite right to tell Tom. Dryden is a

spoilt brat and the sooner some one stops him killing himself, or worse still someone else, the better. In fact I think you can say you have done your good deed for the day.'

Sunday morning came and with the aroma of roast lamb pervading the kitchen, Celia's family descended on Upper Monksford. After they had caught up with the niceties, Julia sent Celia and George into the garden with gin and tonics whilst she gave their daughters, Fiona and Phoebe, jobs to do in the kitchen. Listening with one ear to stories of their sports day and the pop star who opened it, Julia watched their parents sitting under the apple tree opposite Aphrodite.

It was as George took her friend's hands, and holding them whilst leaning forward to kiss his wife, that Celia throwing away her English reserve threw her arms around him and kissed him back; Julia then knew her good deed had not been in vain.

'All's well that ends well,' she spoke aloud.

'Actually we're doing Midsummer Night's Dream next year,' announced Phoebe.

Her elder sister laughed. 'We wanted to do a modern version in an opium den.'

Julia coughed to hide her smile. 'Er, what happened?'

'Miss Higgs-Walker said it was hardly true to life'

Julia laughed, 'Well it would take a bit of believing,' she replied.

The Silence of Aphrodite

Julia Phillips pulled the back door of her cottage firmly shut behind her and walked across the small carefully tendered lawn. On the far side was a wooden seat where after careful inspection of the surface she sat down and regarded her garden with not a little pride.

Her gaze passed over the colourful borders and came to rest on a clematis-adorned statue of Aphrodite. Julia smiled; here she felt was a kindred spirit. Not that she regarded herself as a goddess - let alone the goddess of love. But, she was in love. It was, thought Julia, ironic that here she was, deliriously happy, but unable to broadcast her love, just like the statue of Aphrodite.

Picking up the bag that carried all her paints, she made her way across to the garage on her way to work. By the time she had reached Pencastle's College of Further Education it was almost six thirty, leaving nearly an hour for Julia to set up the still life subject for her students. Her heart beat a little faster as she thought of one in particular. It had been three months ago, on the first evening of term, when a rangy young man had entered her class as a new pupil. From the very moment she had watched him chew the end of his paintbrush, Julia had been attracted to him. Then as she bent over James Bertolli's shoulder and gave him some guidance on his brushwork Julia had been smitten. As his dark hair fell over his eyes he flicked it back with his hand, she thought he reminded her of George Clooney.

He asked her out after the next class and although she may have hesitated for a moment, (after all he could only have been about five years younger than her) she accepted with a slight blush. If she had known how the affair would develop she would probably had gone bright red.

He was an attentive lover and the thought of his mouth softly caressing her body made her sigh with pleasure. He was certainly experienced and Julia's quite adequate knowledge of sex was extended even more, especially as she had been celibate for the nearly two years. Her infatuation knew no bounds, but she did draw the line at making love in a box at the Pencastle's Theatre Royal, especially as the Principle of the College was just below her in the stalls.

It was not until their third meeting outside the hours of college that she found out about his wife. With sinking heart she listened to James's limp explanation and then her hopes were raised as he told her of his impending divorce. He told Julia how badly his wife had treated him and how she belittled him. Then, he told her how much he loved her.

They carried on their affair, meeting regularly once or twice a week, but as he explained, it was better if they kept it as discreet as possible. After all, he mustn't upset the divorce plans. Julia thought of the silent Aphrodite who kept vigilance in her garden.

That evening James arrived earlier than the others and they had a few brief moments before the class assembled. Also that evening Julia had three new students; two were bored housewives who wanted something else to do with their lives, but the third was a talented younger woman, a pretty brunette who turned out to be Italian.

At the break, Julia happened to glance across the room and caught James talking and laughing with the new Italian student, Francesca. With a pang of jealousy she slowly weaved her way over to where they stood sipping coffee. To her dismay they were talking in Italian, a language she had never mastered. James joked about it later that evening, but Julia had an uneasy feeling that he was being a little short with the truth as he tried to explain what they had been talking about.

The following Tuesday, Julia had to go into Pencastle for some shopping and she decided to call into Pan's Coffee House for lunch. As she entered she heard her name being called and glancing over the crowded room espied one of her students waving frantically at her. Smiling tactfully she joined the woman and at her invitation reluctantly took the spare seat. The woman, whom Julia remembered was called Pamela Speake-Patterson, was not her style and she found it difficult to concentrate on her chatter. But she felt her blood rush to her face when the name of James was mentioned. Pamela Speake-Patterson didn't seem to notice, she was just wallowing in gossip; not that it was about Julia and James, but Francesca and James. It appears that they had been seen last Saturday evening in a hotel on the edge of a nearby town. Pamela Speake-Patterson then oozed the details of James's past love life to such an extent that it crossed Julia's mind that maybe Pamela had been a little part of her own sordid stories.

How she stuck out her lunch, Julia will never know. Eventually making her excuses she had left Pamela Speake-Patterson to her own devices whilst she found her car and made her way home. Later sitting in the garden she confided her worst fears to Aphrodite. She felt used, let down with broken promises by James. She admitted that she had been flattered by the younger man and had thoroughly enjoyed their fling. But it hurt that he had not had the decency to tell her it was over, and she had to hear it from another person, particularly Pamela Speake-Patterson. He had lied to her about the divorce, Pamela confided that he had no intention of leaving his wealthy wife. Julia suggested to Aphrodite that James needed to be taught a lesson.

At the next evening class Julia suddenly remembered that she needed a new initiative for her lesson. Remembering her last year's success with stick painting she decided to introduce it to her present class. Using different size twigs, she would give them sepia ink and ask them to choose their own subject. Last year's students came up with a huge range of work including a cocker spaniel, the local castle, a merry-go-round and even a sketch of herself.

It would stretch some of her current students, but it would be good experience and broaden their spectrum. Humming softly to herself she set off down the lane from her house until she reached the copse and plunging into the wooded area she started collecting various sizes of twigs.

Later that evening she mentally patted herself on her back as student after student enthused on her idea. She walked around her class, making comments here and showing techniques there. When she got to James she stood behind him and stared at the naked form on his drawing pad. She had to admit it was good, the young body was given the most desirous of poses and the head…. with a start Julia stared across at Francesca. Seething, she made no comment and passed on to the next student.

Later as Julia sat at her desk she regarded her class with some pride - even James, in between chewing his stick, had produced some excellent work.

She sat with her chin rested on a fist and watched him through narrowed eyes. She thought that he was looking flushed, but it was not until about five minutes had gone by before another student noticed and called out to him.

Bright red, James threw down the twig he had been chewing, his lips were beginning to swell and falling back in his chair he clutched at his throat.

The ambulance was quick and later after all the class had left Julia disposed of all the twigs, only then did she have a twinge of conscience. But it had gone by the next morning when Julia had called the hospital to learn he was out of intensive care. Ringing off, she walked out through the French windows across the lawn to her favourite seat and regarded the smoke from her bonfire of garden rubbish and twigs. How was she to know that James would chew the twig she had given him to use for drawing? After all, none of the others had done so; then of course they weren't given a yew twig. But who would know that? Certainly Aphrodite, who knew her secret.

Lightning Source UK Ltd.
Milton Keynes UK
UKOW04f0502300415
250620UK00001B/5/P